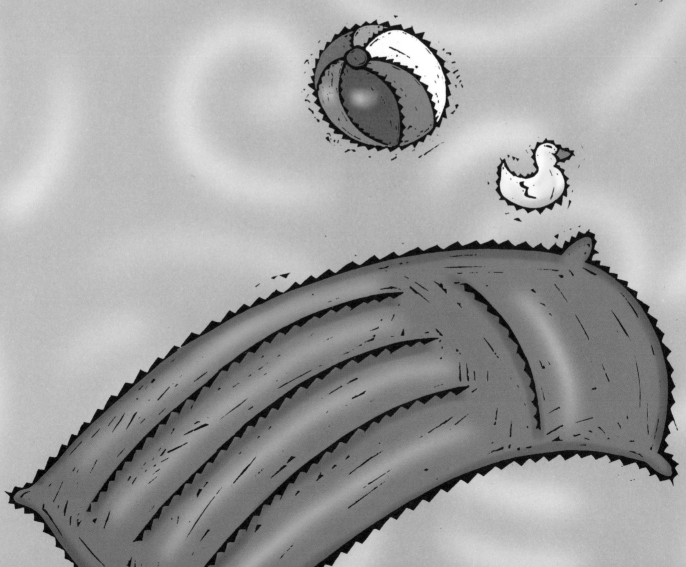

Swimming Lessons

Swimming Lessons

by Betsy Jay

illustrated by Lori Osiecki

rising moon

Books for Young Readers from Northland Publishing

The black line work for the illustrations were done by traditional scratchboard technique,
then the illustrations were scanned and digitally painted in Photoshop.
The text type was set in Eva Antiqua and Tiepolo
The display type was set in Paisley
Composed in the United States of America
Designed by Billie Jo Bishop
Edited by Stephanie Bucholz and Judy Gittenstein
Production Supervised by Lisa Brownfield
Art direction by David Jenney and Rudy Ramos

Manufactured in Hong Kong by Palace Press

FIRST IMPRESSION
ISBN 0-87358-685-9

Library of Congress Catalog Card Number 97-46487
Jay, Betsy, 1978–
Swimming lessons / by Betsy Jay ; illustrated by Lori Osiecki.
p.   cm.
Summary: Although she has found many excuses for refusing to take
swimming lessons, Jane finally faces the inevitable and jumps into
the water for a very good reason.
ISBN 0-87358-685-9
1. Youths' writings, American.   [1. Swimming—Fiction. 2. Fear—
Fiction. 3. Youths' writings.] I. Osiecki, Lori, ill.
II. Title.
PZ7.J3295Sw 1998
[E]—dc21   97-46487

0642/10M/4-98

For my grandmother and Mrs. Cooke. — B. J.

To Max and Alex. — L. O.

One night at supper Momma said to Daddy, "Jane is going to learn to swim this summer." I told Momma I wasn't going to get into any pool. I told her when she took me to the pool to sign up and made me tell the nice lady my name and how old I was.

I told her again when we saw a woman from church at the grocery store and found out that her mean little boy, Jimmy, would be taking swimming lessons, too.

I told her and **told** her, but she just talked about how I wouldn't be scared of the water if I knew how to swim. She said it's very important that I know how to swim, because everyone else she knows who is my age—or who has ever been my age—can swim.

I don't want to know how to swim.

Maybe if I decided to become a sailor  or a fisherman I would need to know how to swim. But I would rather be an elephant rider in the circus, and I don't think they need to know much about swimming. I told Momma that. She said that everyone knows how to swim, including elephant riders, and farmers, and TV repairmen, and even the person who paints the yellow lines on the road.

I don't believe her.

Momma said, "What if you're in a boat and it tips over?"
I said I will never ride in a boat.

She said, "What if Uncle Frank tries to throw you in the pond at the Fourth of July picnic?"

I didn't say anything then because that has a very good chance of happening, and there isn't really any way out once Uncle Frank gets you, except holding your breath for a really, really long time, which might spoil the day for everyone else, even though the ambulance would come and I would get to ride inside it while they saved my life.

Yesterday afternoon Daddy came home from work early and took me to the park. The swimming pool is at the park. We walked by it on the way to the playground. There is a tall fence all the way around it, and only one way in and out. If there was a tidal wave, or a fire, I'm sure somebody would get hurt trying to get out, and it would probably be me. Daddy said there was a lifeguard to make sure everyone was safe and that those things wouldn't happen anyway. I said that you can never be too sure about fires or tidal waves. He said he had never heard of a tidal wave around here, and if there was a fire I could just jump in the pool. I told him it was probably safer to be in a fire than to get in that water.

Momma bought a new bathing suit for me to wear at my swimming lessons. It's pink with a yellow dinosaur on the front that turns purple when you get in the water.

I didn't believe her when she told me. I thought she was trying to trick me, because she said I could only get it wet in the swimming pool, not in the bathtub. I made it wet in the dog's bowl, but only the dinosaur part, and only the dinosaur's tail. I had to work fast while she was talking to Mrs. Henley in the driveway.

Momma wasn't lying. It did turn purple.

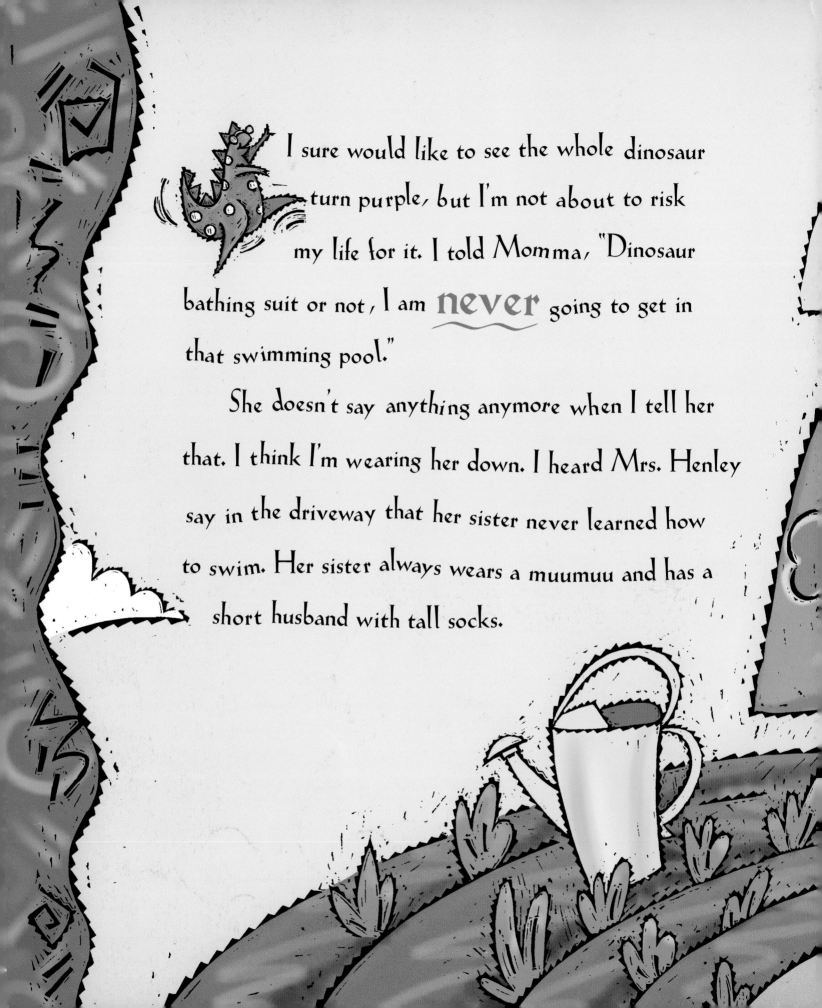

I sure would like to see the whole dinosaur turn purple, but I'm not about to risk my life for it. I told Momma, "Dinosaur bathing suit or not, I am **never** going to get in that swimming pool."

She doesn't say anything anymore when I tell her that. I think I'm wearing her down. I heard Mrs. Henley say in the driveway that her sister never learned how to swim. Her sister always wears a muumuu and has a short husband with tall socks.

Cats never swim at all. They don't like water. I learned this watching television. Cats don't even take baths; they just lick themselves all over. I told this to Momma. She said, "We are not cats, we are people. I said, "I'm not. I'm a cross between a person and a cat. I look like a person on the outside, but I'm a cat on the inside. If you make me get in the water, bad things will happen."

I went outside to find Mrs. Henley's cat to see if it would sit in the birdbath, just to make sure the TV wasn't lying. It wasn't.

On the first day of the swimming lessons Momma put sunscreen all over me. She was worried that it would wash off in the water. She didn't have to worry, I told her, because I am not getting in the swimming pool. I am **not** going to learn how to swim if it's the last thing I do.

I don't care who can swim and who can't. I don't care if I can't become an elephant rider. I don't care if I never see the dinosaur turn purple. I don't care about anything ever again for the rest of my life; I don't care, I'm never going to get in that swimming pool.

Momma said, "Oh, yes you are."

"You can't make me," I said. "You're not my boss," but I should have left that part off.

She pointed her finger at me and told me to go sit on the bleachers until my teacher came, and she didn't want to hear another word. So I went to the bleachers. I was so mad I threw my nose-pinchers. I almost threw them all the way into the water.

Jimmy came over. "I love to swim," he said. "I don't," I told him. Then he told me I was scared because girls can't swim. I told him girls can swim just as good as anybody, probably better than him. "You're a chicken," he said, and I said, "No, I'm not." Then he said, "Chickens and girls can't swim."

That's when the teacher made all of us line up at the side of the pool. She was standing in the water and wanted us to jump in one by one.

Jimmy was first. "On the count of three," she said, but Jimmy jumped in before  she got to three, and then it was my turn. The teacher was counting and time was running out and everyone was looking at me and there was no place to hide. Jimmy was floating in the water making noises like a sick chicken. I got madder and madder and the teacher said, "Three!" and I decided the only way to make everyone stop acting crazy was to jump in, so I did. Jimmy doesn't know **anything** about girls.

I wasn't scared. But everyone else was. It took a long time to get everyone in the water. One little, little girl with a bathing suit just like mine started crying. I showed her my purple dinosaur, and she got in.

That day I learned how to blow bubbles and kick and float. The teacher said I was going to be a good swimmer. Everyone was very proud of me. I don't know why they made such a big deal out of it. Everybody should learn how to swim.

And Jimmy learned some things that day, too. Like anybody can learn to swim if they want to, including girls, and maybe even chickens for all he knows. Even his swimming trunks can swim all by themselves.

But I wouldn't know anything about that.

gone swimming

A MESSAGE FROM THE NATIONAL SAFETY COUNCIL

*O*ver a thousand children, newborn to sixteen years old, drown each year in the United States. But drowning is preventable! Children who learn water safety rules and parents who supervise children when they are near water can help bring the number of deaths by drowning to zero.

The author hopes this story will help remind everyone to be safe in and around water.

—BERT HOOD, *Director of Occupational Safety and Health, Arizona Chapter*

Betsy Jay grew up in Waynesville, North Carolina, with her brother and two sisters. She now attends the University of North Carolina at Asheville, majoring in biology.

Betsy wrote *Swimming Lessons* as an assignment for her twelfth-grade English class. Her teacher liked it so much she encouraged Betsy to try to have it published. Though this is Betsy's first children's book, she has been writing since she was a little girl. Betsy's mom says Jane is a lot like Betsy was when she was little.

Lori Osiecki was born in Shillington, Pennsylvania, and attended the York Academy of Arts. She worked for Hallmark Cards, Inc., for eight years before moving to Arizona and becoming a freelance illustrator. Though she has illustrated books for such educational publishers as Macmillan McGraw-Hill, this is her first children's book to appear on a bookstore shelf.

Lori lives in Mesa, where there are 365 swimming days a year, with her husband Jarek, son Max, daughter Alex, and dog George. Lori was swimming before she could walk, and both her children take swimming lessons—cooperatively—at the Y.